FAST FOOD!

HOUGHTON MIFFLIN COMPANY BOSTON 2001

Walter Lorraine Books

GULP! GULP!

BERNARD
WABER

For Paulis, Rod, Louisa, Dana, and Gary

Many thanks to the numerous teachers and librarians who generously offered cafeteria menus when I, with the prospect of this book in mind, expressed interest in food children favored — from whence came "Foot-long dog" and other delectable listings.

I would also like to express enormous appreciation to Andrew Tarlow, co-owner with Mark Firth of the renowned Diner Restaurant in Williamsburg, Brooklyn, New York, for graciously offering an instructive tour of his kitchen operation and a hands-on demonstration of some of its facilities.

Walter Lorraine (wr) Books

Text copyright © 2001 by Bernard Waber

www.houghtonmifflinbooks.com

Library of Congress Cataloging-in-Publication Data

Waber, Bernard.
    Fast food! gulp! gulp! / by Bernard Waber.
        p. cm.
Summary: All kinds of food is served fast and faster—until the cook has had enough!
    ISBN 0-618-14189-8
    [1. Fast food restaurants—Fiction. 2. Stories in rhyme.] I. Title.
    PZ8.3.W1314 Fas 2001
    [E]—dc21
                                                2001000287

WOZ 10 9 8 7 6 5 4 3 2 1
Printed in the United States of America

"Hurry! Hurry!" shouts Colonel Mane,
owner of a fast food chain.
"Quicker! Quicker!
Step on the gas!
Keep it moving!
Move it fast!

Flip that patty!
Slap it on a bun!

Pile on fries
by the ton!

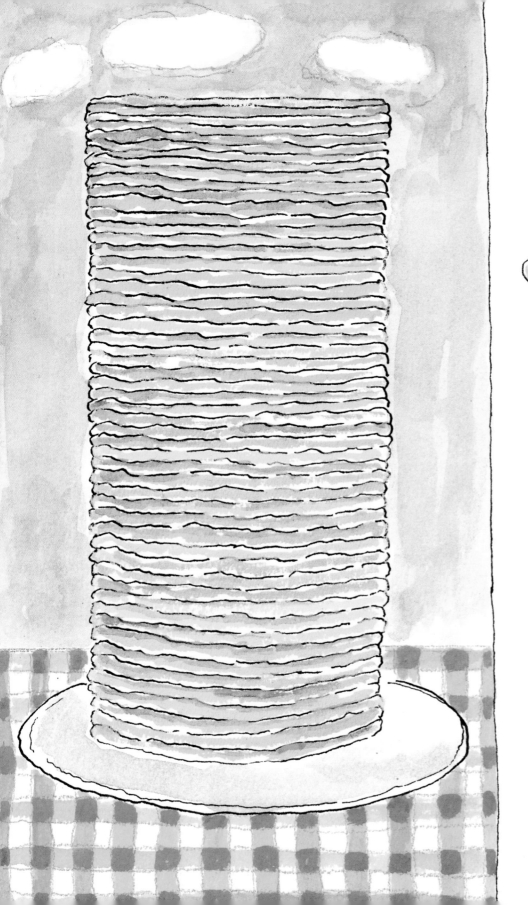

Stack those pancakes
sky-high!

Twirl and hurl
that pizza pie!"

7

FAST FOOD! GULP! GULP!

Munch! Munch!
Crunch! Crunch!
Chew! Chew!
Chomp! Chomp!

Oink! Oink!
Grunt! Grunt!
Quack! Quack!
Snack! Snack!

Pick! Pick!
Lick! Lick!
Slurp! Slurp!
Burp! Burp!

DOWN!
DOWN!

Things are hopping!
Things are popping
in Fast Food Town.

We are the kitchen's
fast food crew.

Hustling and bustling
are what we do.

I cook.

I chop.

I wrap.

I mop.

I serve.

I groan.

13

I work the phone.
"Take-out line!
Hello! Hello!

Sloppy Joe.
Malted to go.

Super club.
Meatball sub.

14

Tuna boat.
Ice cream float.

Philly steak.
Frosty shake.

15

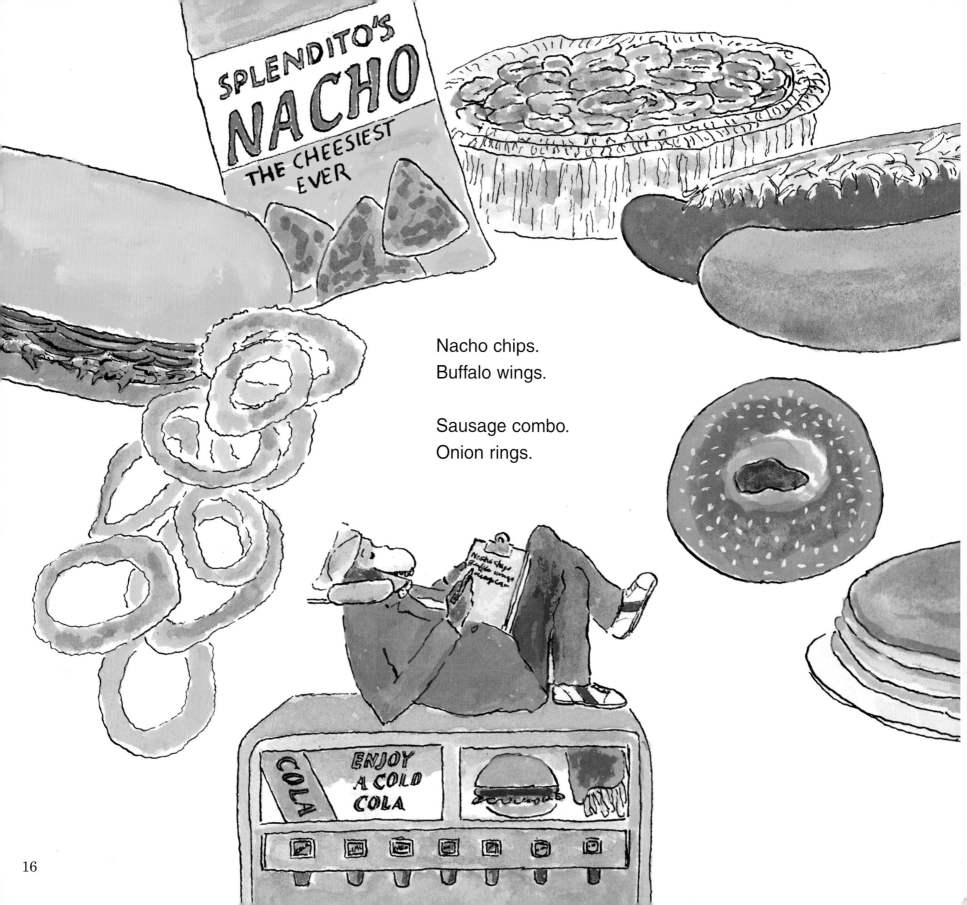

Nacho chips.
Buffalo wings.

Sausage combo.
Onion rings.

16

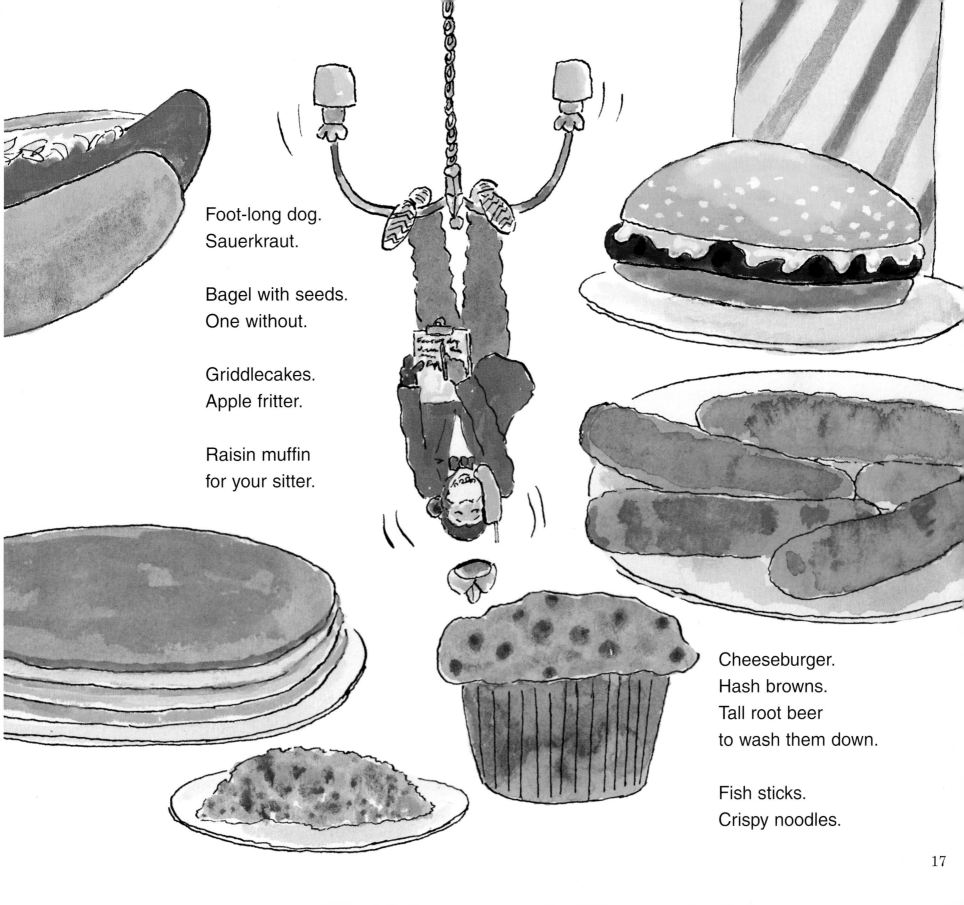

Foot-long dog.
Sauerkraut.

Bagel with seeds.
One without.

Griddlecakes.
Apple fritter.

Raisin muffin
for your sitter.

Cheeseburger.
Hash browns.
Tall root beer
to wash them down.

Fish sticks.
Crispy noodles.

Hush puppies
for your poodles?

Take-out line.
Hello! Hello!
Goodbye! Goodbye!
It's time to go."

Folks, meet Jiffy Jack,
big-shot boss
on the fast food track.
Now Jack serves meals,
he reckons,
you can eat
in thirty seconds.

FAST FOOD!
GULP! GULP!

Munch! Munch!
Crunch! Crunch!
Chew! Chew!
Chomp! Chomp!
Oink! Oink!
Grunt! Grunt!

FOOD COURT

Quack! Quack!
Snack! Snack!
Pick! Pick!
Lick! Lick!

Slurp! Slurp!
Burp! Burp!

**DOWN!
DOWN!**

Got to get a slice
of Fast Food Town.

21

FASTEST FOOD in THE WEST
ALSO NORTH, SOUTH and EAST

LONE CAT'S

Folks, meet fast food's
Lone Cat Mewing,
who rustles up meals
you can eat
without chewing.

23

"That's it! I quit!"

24

"Uh, oh! Cook just quit."   "Got into a snit."   "Began to pout."

"Then walked out."   "Left in a huff."   "Yelled, 'Had enough of . . .

25

FAST FOOD!
GULP! GULP!

Munch! Munch!
Crunch! Crunch!
Chew! Chew!
Chomp! Chomp!
Oink! Oink!
Grunt! Grunt!
Quack! Quack!
Snack! Snack!
Pick! Pick!
Lick! Lick!
Slurp! Slurp!
Burp! Burp!

DOWN!
DOWN!

And all that
hustling and bustling
around."

Soooooo–

after Cook said goodbye
to the fast food pace . . .

she got herself a job
in a health food place,
slowly preparing
nature's greenery . . .

Veg

WE OFFER
TAKE-OUT
PICNIC
LUNCHES

29

for folks taking time
to enjoy the scenery.

Tweet! Tweet!
Bon appétit—
whatever you eat.